THE REAL MOTHER GOOSE COLORING BOOK

RENDERED BY
STEPHEN V. GACHE

BASED ON THE ILLUSTRATIONS BY
BLANCHE FISHER WRIGHT

DOVER PUBLICATIONS
GARDEN CITY, NEW YORK

NOTE

Mother Goose and her timeless collection of rhymes are within this coloring book, waiting for you to bring them to life. Each page contains a different rhyme, plus a black and white image rendered from Blanche Fisher Wright's *The Real Mother Goose*—the most famous collection of these enduring verses ever printed! Children will delight in the lively rhythm and nonsense of each rhyme, and adults will reminisce with these classic staples of childhood. Use your imagination as you add color to Georgy Porgy, Peter Pumpkin-Eater, Little Tom Tucker, Humpty Dumpty, and other memorable Mother Goose characters, then read the rhymes aloud for even more fun!

Copyright

Copyright © 2009 by Dover Publications
All rights reserved.

Bibliographical Note

The Real Mother Goose Coloring Book is a new work, first published by Dover Publications in 2009.

International Standard Book Number

ISBN-13: 978-0-486-46991-1
ISBN-10: 0-486-46991-3

Manufactured in the United States of America
46991307   2023
www.doverpublications.com

LUCY LOCKET

Lucy Locket lost her pocket,
Kitty Fisher found it;
Nothing in it, nothing in it,
But the binding round it.

THE CAT AND THE FIDDLE

Hey, diddle, diddle!
The cat and the fiddle,
The cow jumped over the moon;
The little dog laughed
To see such sport,
And the dish ran away with the spoon.

2

GEORGY PORGY

Georgy Porgy, pudding and pie,
Kissed the girls and made them cry.
When the boys came out to play,
Georgy Porgy ran away.

GOOSEY, GOOSEY, GANDER

Goosey, goosey, gander,
    Whither dost thou wander?
Upstairs and downstairs
    And in my lady's chamber.

There I met an old man
    Who wouldn't say his prayers;
I took him by the left leg,
    And threw him down the stairs.

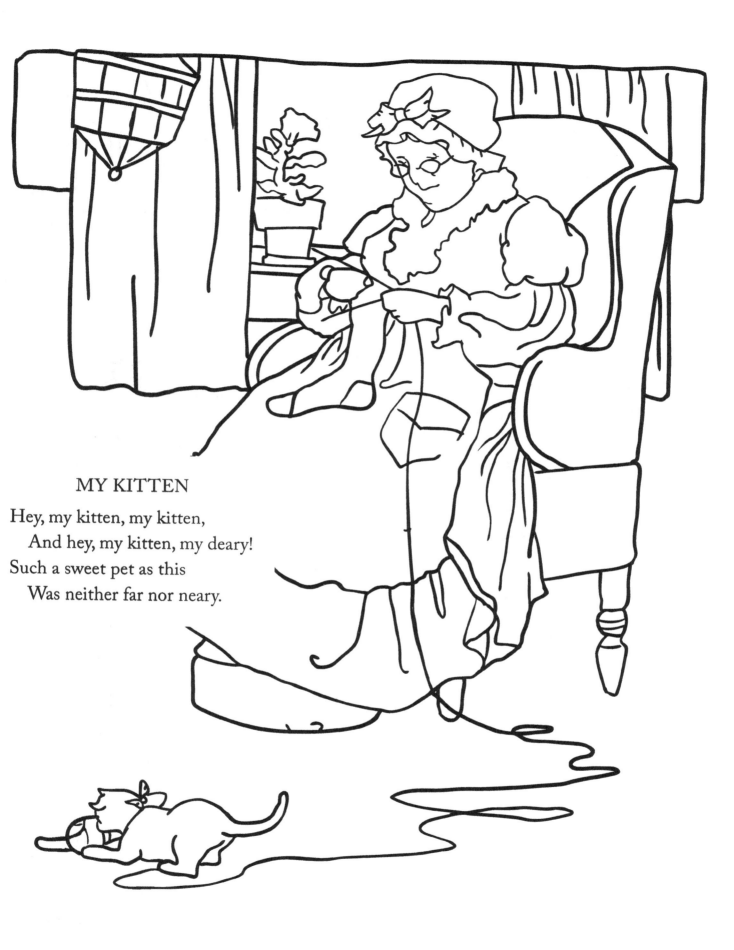

MY KITTEN

Hey, my kitten, my kitten,
    And hey, my kitten, my deary!
Such a sweet pet as this
    Was neither far nor neary.

BAA, BAA, BLACK SHEEP

Baa, baa, black sheep,
Have you any wool?
Yes, marry, have I,
Three bags full;

One for my master,
One for my dame,
But none for the little boy
Who cries in the lane.

HUSH-A-BYE

Hush-a-bye, baby, on the tree top!
When the wind blows the cradle
    will rock;
When the bough breaks the cradle
    will fall;
Down will come baby, bough, cradle
    and all.

OLD WOMAN, OLD WOMAN

There was an old woman tossed in a basket,
  Seventeen times as high as the moon;
But where she was going no mortal could tell,
  For under her arm she carried a broom.

"Old woman, old woman, old woman," said I,
  "Whither, oh whither, oh whither so high?"
"To sweep the cobwebs from the sky;
  And I'll be with you by-and-by."

LADYBIRD

Ladybird, ladybird, fly away home!
Your house is on fire, your children
    all gone,
All but one, and her name is Ann,
And she crept under the pudding
    pan.

MARY, MARY, QUITE
CONTRARY

Mary, Mary, quite contrary,
    How does your garden grow?
Silver bells and cockle-shells,
    And pretty maids all of a row.

PAT-A-CAKE

Pat-a-cake, pat-a-cake,
    Baker's man!
So I do, master,
    As fast as I can.

Pat it, and prick it,
    And mark it with T,
Put it in the oven
    For Tommy and me.

THE PUMPKIN-EATER

Peter, Peter, pumpkin-eater,
Had a wife and couldn't keep her;
He put her in a pumpkin shell,
And there he kept her very well.

PEASE PORRIDGE

Pease porridge hot,
  Pease porridge cold,
Pease porridge in the pot,
  Nine days old.
Some like it hot,
  Some like it cold,
Some like it in the pot,
  Nine days old.

13

THE TARTS

The Queen of Hearts,
She made some tarts,
All on a summer's day;
The Knave of Hearts,
He stole the tarts,
And took them clean away.

The King of Hearts
Called for tarts,
And beat the Knave full sore;
The Knave of Hearts
Brought back the tarts,
And vowed he'd steal no more.

LITTLE TOM TUCKER

Little Tom Tucker
 Sings for his supper.
What shall he eat?
 White bread and butter.
How will he cut it
 Without e'er a knife?
How will he be married
 Without e'er a wife?

15

YOUNG ROGER AND DOLLY

Young Roger came tapping at
    Dolly's window,
    Thumpaty, thumpaty, thump!

He asked for admittance; she
    answered him "No!"
    Frumpaty, Frumpaty, Frump!

"No, no, Roger, no! as you came
    you may go!"
    Stumpaty, stumpaty, stump!

WHEN

When I was
a bachelor
I lived by
myself;
And all the
bread and
cheese I got
I laid upon the
shelf.

The rats and the mice
They made such a strife,
I was forced to go to London
To buy me a wife.

The streets were so bad,
And the lanes were so narrow,
I was forced to bring my wife home
In a wheelbarrow.

The wheelbarrow broke,
And my wife had a fall;
Down came wheelbarrow,
Little wife and all.

17

MARY'S LAMB

Mary had a little lamb,
    Its fleece was white as snow;
And everywhere that Mary went
    The lamb was sure to go.

He followed her to school one day;
    Which was against the rule;
It made the children laugh and play
    To see a lamb at school.

And so the teacher turned him out,
    But still he lingered near,
And waited patiently about
    Till Mary did appear.

Then he ran to her, and laid
    His head upon her arm,
As if he said, "I'm not afraid,—
    You'll keep me from all harm."

"What makes the lamb love Mary so?"
    The eager children cry.
"Oh, Mary loves the lamb, you know,"
    The teacher did reply.

And you each gentle animal
    In confidence may bind,
And make it follow at your will,
    If you are only kind.

THE BUNCH OF BLUE RIBBONS

Oh, dear, what can the matter be?
Oh, dear, what can the matter be?
Oh, dear, what can the matter be?
 Johnny's so long at the fair.

He promised he'd buy me a bunch
 of blue ribbons,
He promised he'd buy me a bunch
 of blue ribbons,
He promised he'd buy me a bunch
 of blue ribbons,
 To tie up my bonny brown hair.

TO MARKET

To market, to market, to buy a fat
    pig,

Home again, home again, jiggety jig.

To market, to market, to buy a fat
    hog,

Home again, home again, jiggety
    jog.

To market, to market, to buy a plum
    bun,

Home again, home again, market is
    done.

JACK

Jack be nimble, Jack be
quick,
Jack jump over the candle-
stick.

SEE-SAW

See-saw, Margery Daw,
Sold her bed and lay upon straw.

CURLY-LOCKS

Curly-locks, Curly-locks, wilt thou be mine?

Thou shalt not wash the dishes, nor yet feed
    the swine;

But sit on a cushion, and sew a fine seam,

And feed upon strawberries, sugar, and
    cream.

HUMPTY DUMPTY

Humpty Dumpty sat on a wall,

Humpty Dumpty had a great fall;

All the King's horses, and all the
King's men

Cannot put Humpty Dumpty
together again.

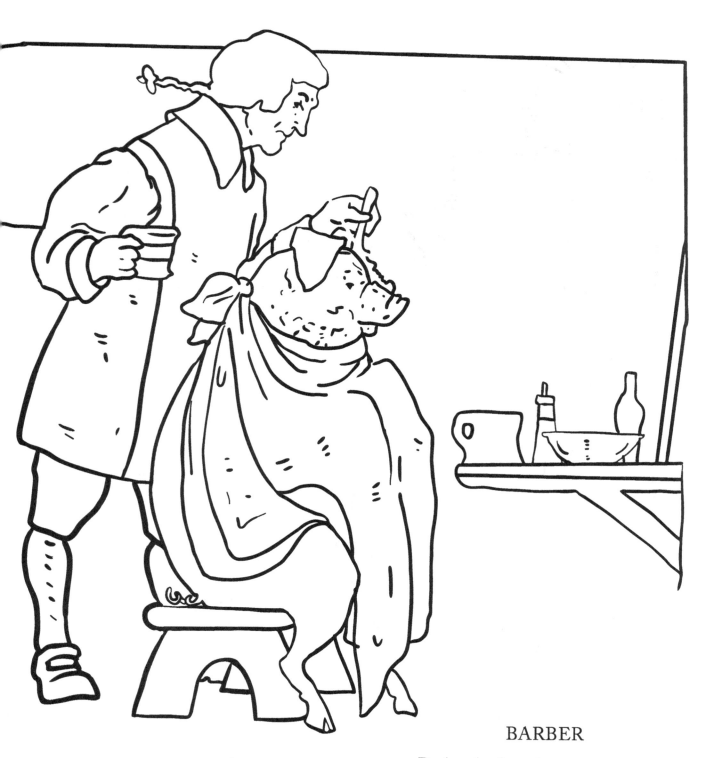

BARBER

Barber, barber, shave a pig.
How many hairs will make a wig?
Four and twenty; that's enough.
Give the barber a pinch of snuff.

THE OLD WOMAN AND THE PEDLAR

There was an old woman, as I've heard tell,
She went to market her eggs for to sell;
She went to market all on a market-day,
And she fell asleep on the King's highway.

There came by a pedlar whose name was Stout,
He cut her petticoats all round about;
He cut her petticoats up to the knees,
Which made the old woman to shiver and freez

When the little old woman first did wake,
She began to shiver and she began to shake;
She began to wonder and she began to cry,
"Lauk a mercy on me, this can't be I!

"But if it be I, as I hope it be,
I've a little dog at home, and he'll know me;
If it be I, he'll wag his little tail,
And if it not be I, he'll loudly bark and wail."

Home went the little woman all in the dark;
Up got the little dog, and he began to bark;
He began to bark, so she began to cry,
"Lauk a mercy on me, this is none of I!"

FOREHEAD, EYES,
HEEKS, NOSE, MOUTH,
AND CHIN

ere sits the Lord Mayor,
  Here sits his two men,
ere sits the cock,
  Here sits the hen,
ere sit the little chickens,
  Here they run in.
in-chopper, chin-chopper,
  chin-chopper, chin!

THREE BLIND MICE

Three blind mice! See how they run!

They all ran after the farmer's wife,

Who cut off their tails with a
 carving knife.

Did you ever see such a thing in
 your life

As three blind mice?

BANBURY CROSS

de a cock-horse to Banbury Cross,

see an old lady upon a white
horse.

ngs on her fingers, and bells on
her toes,

e shall have music wherever she
goes.

29

PUSSY-CAT AND QUEEN

"Pussy-cat, pussy-cat,
　　Where have you been?"
"I've been to London
　　To look at the Queen."

"Pussy-cat, pussy-cat,
　　What did you there?"
"I frightened a little mouse
　　Under the chair."